**WRITTEN AND ILLUSTRATED
BY MATTY MITCHELL**

Hazel, I hope you stay as adventurous as you are right now.

Mum, thanks for encouraging me to dream my dreams.

www.mattymitchellbooks.com
Email: mm@mattymitchellbooks.com
Instagram: @MattyMitchellbooks

Copyright © 2018 by 38 Ladders Publishing, LLC

All rights reserved. No part of this book may be reproduced or transmitted in any form or by any means, electronic or mechanical, including photocopying, recording or by any information storage and retrieval without permission in writing from the publisher.

Published by 38 Ladders Publishing, LLC

ISBN-13: 978-0-9862178-3-8

Printed in U.S.A

HAVE YOU MET LONNIE LEFT FOOT?

No? Well, Lonnie's excited to meet you and take you on the next adventurous adventure. What you need to know about Lonnie is that he has a wild imagination and it's fueled by his ability to build just about anything. Lonnie is usually sporting goggles, but not because he has bad vision. His goggles are enhanced with the latest sock technology (and he reckons they make him look super cool).

HAVE YOU MET ROGER RIGHT FOOT?

Maybe? Well, Roger can't wait for you to join him on this next adventure. What you need to know about Roger is that he is not really an adventure seeker, but he's willing to say yes to most adventures that come his way, especially when it's for his mate Lonnie. And boy, does Lonnie seem to get Roger into some interesting situations. Roger is very proud of the patch on his right side, but that is a story for another time.

HERE ARE THE ITEMS FOR YOUR TIME TRAVEL ADVENTURE.

THE ULTRA WATCH:
The watch does many things, but you only need to worry about 3 of the functions.

1. Tracks where Theodore is and beeps the closer you get to him.
2. Stays in contact with me through the space-time continuum.
3. It looks socktastic.

THE STRETCHATRON 3000:
I created the stretchiest rubber band the world has ever seen.

THE LASSO-IEST SHOE LACE:
Honestly, I just tied it into a lasso so you didn't have to.

THE BIO DUCT TAPE:
I made this crazy sticky duct tape, which also happens to be biodegradable.

THE POWER BAG
It's a bag with a cool name.

THE SUPERIOR FORK:
Made of the strongest material known to sock kind. And it can be used for climbing, digging or getting to that itchy spot on your stitching you can never reach.

Made in the USA
Lexington, KY
27 January 2018